LUTON LIBRARIES

Renewals, online accounts, catalogue searches,
eBooks and other online services:

https://arena.yourlondonlibrary.net/web/luton/

Renewals: 01582 547413, (24hr) 0333 370 4700

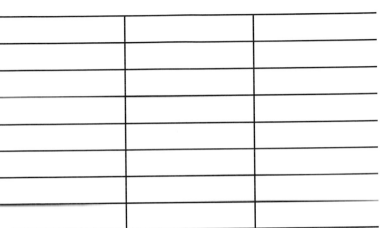

**Luton
Culture**

Read more in the Evie's Magic Bracelet series!

Evie's Magic Bracelet

The Fire Bird

JESSICA ENNIS-HILL

and Elen Caldecott

Illustrated by
Erica-Jane Waters

Hodder
Children's
Books

HODDER CHILDREN'S BOOKS

First published in Great Britain in 2018 by Hodder and Stoughton

1 3 5 7 9 10 8 6 4 2

Text and illustrations copyright © Jessica Ennis Limited, 2018

A CIP catalogue record for this book
is available from the British Library.

ISBN 978 1 444 93444 1

Printed and bound in Great Britain
by Clays Ltd, St Ives plc

The paper and board used in this book
are made from wood from responsible sources

MIX
Paper from
responsible sources
FSC
www.fsc.org   FSC® C104740

Hodder Children's Books
An imprint of
Hachette Children's Group
Part of Hodder and Stoughton
Carmelite House
50 Victoria Embankment
London EC4Y 0DZ

An Hachette UK Company
www.hachette.co.uk

www.hachettechildrens.co.uk

To Myla
Our lovely crazy chocolate Labrador x
– J.E-H.

To Bertie, by himself
– E.C.

Chapter 1

As far as Evie Hall was concerned, a stop-over at Isabelle's house was as exciting as fireworks at an ice show. But the packing to get ready was a very serious business. She liked to be prepared, ready for anything. And people who forget to take their toothbrush on an overnight stay were NOT ready for anything. She had a list of all the things she wanted to take and she ticked them off carefully – toothbrush, toothpaste, clean clothes for the morning, Snookums her teddy bear (for her eyes only), and pyjamas.

Magic light fizzed like mini sparklers above her backpack. There was always a little explosion of magic whenever anyone was happy. She and her friends, Isabelle and Ryan, could see magic all the time thanks to a gift from a unicorn. It glittered, golden in the air. But they could only use magic with help from Grandma Iris. The bracelets she sent from her home in Jamaica, all the way to Sheffield, allowed Evie to use magic for three whole days.

There was one other thing that she wished she could take to make a stop-over at Isabelle's totally, completely perfect, and that was a magic bracelet from Grandma Iris.

She had a little wooden tree on her bedside cabinet that kept her old bracelets safe – they hung from its little branches like teensy tinsel. She grinned. Never mind. She would just have to have fun with Isabelle and Ryan without magic. It was half term, after all, and the days were going to be packed with trips out to places like the swimming baths and museums. She'd spend time with her friends, and her little sister Lily (no way to escape her!), and the rest of her family. She couldn't be mardy just because there was no magic.

She was zipping up her bag when she heard Myla, the dog, barking at the front door. Evie's room was up in the attic, under the sloping roof and skylight, so she had to peer over the banister to see what Myla was barking at. Mum had opened the door, and was holding a parcel. A parcel wrapped in beautiful paper, tied with a ribbon. A parcel that looked a lot like …

'Evie,' Mum called up, 'there's something come in the post for you.'

Hurray! Hurray! Evie jigged up and down, before pelting down the stairs with a superhero cape of magic flying behind her.

It was a bracelet from Grandma Iris. It had to be!

Moments later, she was alone in the front room, with the door closed. She unwrapped the parcel carefully, and inside, nestled in tissue paper, was a beautiful new bracelet. Its beads were blue and white, like wisps of clouds in the sky on a sunny day.

Usually, Grandma Iris sent a note with every bracelet. The note had clues about the type of magic that the bracelet could do. But, mostly, the clues were too tricksy to guess. It was Grandma Iris' little joke that the instructions weren't instructions at all!

Evie pulled the note free and read it:

Sensible girls keep their feet on the ground,
But who wants to be grounded when there's magic around?
Sometimes you have to let yourself go,
Relax, unwind, go with the flow.

Hmm. Evie flipped the note over, but the other side was blank. She was to let herself go? But why? And how? And why would

she be grounded? She hardly ever got into trouble. Well, not on purpose, anyway.

There was only one way to find out what the bracelet did, and that was to try it out. She slipped it on to her wrist, and turned it, once, twice, three times.

A snake of gold light burst from the bracelet and twisted around her arm. Magic! She looked gleefully around the room. What had happened? What had changed?

She couldn't spot any difference.

The magic must have done something. But she couldn't tell what. Odd.

'Evie, do you want that lift to Isabelle's?' Mum called from the hall. 'Mum-and-Dad's taxis are ready.'

Evie smiled and folded up the wrapping paper. She didn't know what the bracelet did, but she would work it out. Then, she and Isabelle and Ryan could have fun tonight at the stop-over!

Mum dropped her off outside Isabelle's house, and waited in the car to make sure she got inside safely. Evie gave a huge wave once Isabelle opened the door. Mum blew a kiss and drove away.

Isabelle's house was the same as Evie's from the outside: a red brick house with neighbours stuck to it on either side. But, inside, it was a different story. Isabelle's dad was a builder and he had knocked down walls, and put in loads of glass and shiny metal and pale wood, so that the whole ground floor looked like something from a posh magazine. Isabelle and her big sister had a playroom, just off the kitchen.

'Come in, come in, come in,' Isabelle squealed. 'Put your bag down. Ryan's here already. I've got cupcakes and the trampoline is out and Dad's just put up my new present – well, mine and Lizzie's present – you'll never-guess-in-a-million-years what it is!'

Her friend helped Evie off with her
backpack and dropped it casually on the hall
floor. Evie paused – her parents would go
spare if she dropped stuff about the house.
But the rules were different everywhere; it
was confusing sometimes. Isabelle's dark
eyes sparkled in excitement as she pulled
Evie through the hall. Her mum was making
herself a cuppa in the kitchen. Evie waved,
and thought it was probably polite to
stop and say hello, but Isabelle was like a
runaway train, hurtling down her tracks, so
the wave was all Evie could manage.

'Lizzie asked Dad for it. The present. I
wasn't sure, because of maths, but it's ace.'

Maths?

What on earth was Isabelle talking about?

The playroom, off the sparkling kitchen, was painted in bright colours and had purple and red beanbags dotted about the floor. There was a big telly on the wall, and a mini football table. Evie couldn't help thinking, not for the first time, that Isabelle was very, very lucky.

Ryan was standing in the centre of the room. Which was weird. But Evie soon realised what he was up to. Isabelle's new present was on the wall opposite the telly, and he was getting ready to play – it was a dartboard! 'Check this!' Ryan said. He took aim and threw the dart. It landed with a thunk in the red dot in the centre of the board. 'I'm a natural!'

'Wow,' Evie said, 'isn't that a bit, well, dangerous?' She said that mostly because the wall around the dartboard was covered in lots of tiny holes, like the noticeboard at school. Someone around here wasn't a natural.

Isabelle grinned. 'Isn't it brilliant? Here, you have to stand behind the line. Ryan, give her the darts.'

Isabelle manoeuvred Evie into position, pulling and pushing her so that her toes were directly behind a white line taped to the floor. Isabelle kept both hands on Evie's shoulders and kept an eagle eye on her feet, to make sure there was no cheating.

Then, she stopped.

And dropped down to the ground, on her knees.

Evie looked down at the back of Isabelle's head in confusion. 'What's up? What's wrong?'

Isabelle's face was right down near the ground. She peered at Evie's shoes like a scientist peering down a particularly interesting microscope.

'Evie,' Isabelle said, 'I don't mean to worry you, or anything, but there's something weird going on with your feet. Evie, you're floating.'

Chapter
2

Ryan dropped down next to Isabelle. They were both staring at Evie's feet.

'It's true,' Ryan said. 'Your feet aren't touching the floor.'

Evie bent double to get a closer look. She could see a little sliver of light under her shoes, just a millimetre or two. She felt

normal. But she definitely wasn't touching
the ground any more.

'Did you, by any chance, get a present this
morning?' Ryan asked.

Of course!

Evie felt her grin spread like butter on
warm toast. She remembered the riddle,
'Who wants to be grounded when there's
magic around?'. It wasn't grounded like
being in trouble, it was grounded like being
on the ground! Grandma Iris had sent a
bracelet that let her float … or fly?

Evie bounced up into the air. She came
back down, but very slowly, as though she
was light as a feather.

'Wow!' Ryan said.

It felt very odd, but cool. Almost as if the air around her was thick enough to hold her up. It felt like falling into jelly.

'How high can you go?' Isabelle asked curiously.

The playroom ceiling was quite low, painted a creamy-white like cheesecake. Could she touch it, if she tried?

Evie bent her knees and launched upwards. She sailed swiftly, like a dart, and clattered into the ceiling. She pressed her hands against the roof to stop her head bumping hard. She floated back down to the ground gently.

'You look like those videos of people on the space station,' Isabelle said. They'd watched an amazing one on the internet of an astronaut floating themselves around their space home by pulling and pushing themselves off walls.

That was exactly what it felt like.

'Woo-hoo!' Evie said and kicked off from the floor again. But this time she fell back down with a very ordinary thump.

'More magic,' Isabelle said. 'You need a boost of more magic.'

Evie twisted the bracelet on her wrist three times. It burst with glittering magic and Evie was able to launch herself upwards again. This time she was able to control it better, and, instead of hitting the ceiling, she glided across the room gracefully. She sailed right over the table football and landed with bent knees on the other side.

'Can I have a turn?' Ryan asked.

'Of course.' Evie liked them all to share in the magical adventures; she'd learned it was better that way.

Ryan put on the bracelet and, with a sprinkling of gold, he did a slow and careful spin in midair, then floated to lie gently on the ceiling.

It was funny looking at him from underneath, with his blond hair falling towards them. It made the world feel wibbly.

When he came back down, it was Isabelle's turn. She swam across the room, giggling as she did an elegant breaststroke in the air. 'This is amazing!' she said. 'The best bracelet ever. We can fly!'

Evie could hardly believe it. It was wonderful, like a dream.

Isabelle landed neatly at Evie's side. Then, she took Evie's hand. The magic flowed over

them both and they both took to the air,
swooping and gliding together. It was tricky
to manoeuvre in midair, what with there
being two of them. They had to keep their
arms and legs balanced – and Evie held very
tight to Isabelle's hand. She didn't want to
let go and fall to the ground with a painful
thump.

Ryan grabbed her free hand as they
swooped close to him. His feet lifted from
the ground and all three were up in the air
together.

But there wasn't enough room in the
playroom for all three of them to turn.

The far wall got closer and closer.

'Left!' Isabelle yelled.

'Right!' Ryan shouted.

Evie didn't know what to do. She tried to roll forward, like turning in a swimming pool, but her arm got twisted and tangled in Isabelle's.

They all three whumped into the wall.

The dartboard fell to the floor. Ryan fell beside it. Isabelle landed on top of him. Evie slid down on her back.

'Ow!' someone said.

Evie agreed. 'Ow! I'm bruised purple,' she said. She limped to her feet. The others crawled up too.

The playroom door opened. Isabelle's mum stood in the doorway looking concerned. 'What was that noise?' she said.

Her eyes landed on the fallen dartboard. 'Oh dear, did it fall off the wall? I wondered if the nail was strong enough. No more darts until I've fixed it properly. Understood?'

They all nodded weakly.

Evie rubbed her hip where it had crashed into the plaster. No darts was the least of her worries!

Isabelle's mum left and pulled the door closed behind her.

Ryan picked up the dartboard and the stray darts and put them on the table football. 'Shame,' he said, 'I was just getting good.'

'You've just found out you can fly, Ryan,' Isabelle said, rolling her eyes at him. 'That's worth stopping a game for, isn't it?'

'Good point,' he said.

'But there isn't really enough room in here to see what we can do,' Evie said sadly.

Isabelle moved to the big glass door that slid aside to let people into the garden. The sun was shining, and, though it was a bit chilly, she opened it. Isabelle looked up at the blue sky with wisps of white cloud.

Evie knew exactly what Isabelle was thinking. She wanted to fly right out of the house and hover over the High Street waving at passers-by. It was just Isabelle's style. 'We can't,' Evie said. 'We can fly, but we're not invisible! Someone will be bound to see us. In fact, everyone will see us!'

It was easy to read Isabelle's face. Her expression went from disagreeing, to disappointed, then disagreeing again.

'Isabelle!' Evie tried again. 'We can't! We'll get caught. And then everyone will know about Grandma Iris' bracelets.'

Isabelle put her hands on her hips. She was still wearing the bracelet and Evie could see the blue beads twinkle in the sunshine.

'We can't now,' Isabelle agreed. 'It's totally the wrong time of day. But tonight, well, that will be different.'

'Tonight?' Ryan asked.

'Yes! Just think of it. As soon as the sun sets, we can swoop off into the sky. We can sail over the lights of the city, with the streetlights like rows of sparkling pearls below us. We can fly over the school, and the park, and even off into the hills if we want. It will be amazing.'

Evie could picture it now – the city like a beautiful carpet of lights below them. And, at night, no one would even notice.

'Let's do it,' she whispered.

Chapter 3

Evie could hardly wait for the night to come
so that they could really fly, but the rest of
the day was fun too. Isabelle's mum fixed
the dartboard, so they played lots of darts
– they all got better at hitting the board,
not the wall, and Isabelle's maths got a tiny
bit better too. They ate snacks and played

on the trampoline in the garden. But Evie's mind kept wandering back to the bracelet and all the fun they would have as soon as the sun set.

They were yawning and rubbing their eyes, with their teeth cleaned, at eight o'clock.

'What's up with you lot?' Isabelle's mum asked. 'I normally have to staple you all into bed at gone ten!'

Evie stretched her arms above her head and gave the biggest yawn she could manage. 'It's been a tiring sort of day,' she said.

Isabelle caught her eye and they both tried hard not to giggle.

'Well, if you insist. Goodnight, all,'
Isabelle's mum said.

Evie and Ryan both had inflatable
mattresses and sleeping bags set up on the
floor of Isabelle's room. But they didn't
get into bed. Instead, all three sat near the
window, waiting until the house got quiet.
They heard Isabelle's sister, Lizzie, close her
bedroom door. 'She'll be chatting on the
internet for hours,' Isabelle whispered. They
heard the sound of the news begin on the
telly downstairs. 'Mum and Dad won't move
until it's over,' Isabelle said.

It was time.

Isabelle opened her bedroom window
slowly, so as not to attract unwanted

attention from nosy big sisters, or curious parents. The sky was stormy sea blue, with the first few stars twinkling shyly. Below, the bushes and plants in Isabelle's garden were coal black shapes. The garden backed on to the neighbours' and the row of terraces opposite. Lights were on in some of the bedroom windows, but the curtains were pulled across – red, purple, orange, green, like dragons' scales sparkling in the night.

There was just enough room for all three of them to sit on the windowsill, with their slippered feet swaying in the cool night air. Evie was in the middle, with her hand on her bracelet. 'Are we sure about this?' She peered down. It wasn't a long drop on to the kitchen roof, she didn't think they would hurt themselves if the magic didn't work for some reason. But, really, she didn't want to find out.

'Don't worry,' Isabelle said, 'the magic won't let us down.'

'Let's hope it keeps us up,' Ryan said with a grin.

Evie twisted the bracelet. Gold light floated free, glittering like flame. She reached for Isabelle and Ryan's hand. 'One, two, three ...'

They leaned forwards, tipping off the sill … and glided into the air, like pushing off the edge at the swimming baths! Evie held her breath. It was just like jumping into water! And, just like in water, she found herself bobbing and floating next to her friends!

'Don't let go,' Isabelle squeaked. Evie gripped her friends' hands tight. Then she kicked with her legs and all three surged up and away from the house. They were above the roofs, looking down on tiles and chimney pots. A cat mewled from atop a fence. Somewhere a dog barked in reply. But they were surging up and up and up.

'Woo-hoo!' Ryan yelled. He held his free

arm out, trailing his fingers through wisps of cloud. 'This is amazing!'

Evie soon learned that she could lean her body one way, then the other, to change direction. They swooped high over the park and the city farm and even their school. The city was below them now, the roads were ribbons of light. Shops spilled friendly glows on to dark pavements. A few lit windows in the office blocks in the city showed there were still people hard at work; from up in the sky the bright windows were like fairy lights wrapped around a pole. Air rushed past Evie's ears, with a whooshing sound. Somewhere, in the clouds above, they heard the roar of an aeroplane engine.

'Careful,' Isabelle laughed, 'not too high.'

Evie set a course closer to the ground. The trees looked like broccoli stems, the people like grains of rice. They followed the river north, it was like an ink spill across the ground. They reached the outskirts of the city, past the football ground and Hillsborough Park. Evie risked taking them lower. Hopefully it was too dark to be spotted and she loved seeing Sheffield spread out below like goodies on a picnic blanket.

'Flying is my new favourite thing,' she said. 'It's brilliant!'

They were gliding above a parish church when Ryan pointed down to something. 'What's that?' he asked.

Evie tried to make it out. There was a
silver weather vane on top of the church
steeple, in the shape of a cockerel. But it
wasn't that that had caught Ryan's attention.
There was something hunched over the
weather vane, something strange. She flew
them closer. The beast – she thought that
because it was definitely an animal – was
clinging to the metal, its huge arms wrapped
tight around it. No. That wasn't right, she
realised. They weren't arms, they were
wings, its wings were wrapped around the
metal pole.

'Is it an eagle?' Isabelle asked.

Evie had never heard of an eagle in
Sheffield, but the bird was big enough to be

one. They were only a short distance away
now, swooping over a late night kebab shop
where the sound of dance music blared. She
headed for the quiet of the churchyard. They
hovered above a yew tree, before coming
to settle on the topmost branch. It creaked
underneath them, but held their weight.

The bird was dark against the skyline,
but Evie could see the elegant sweep of a
long tail and a crest of feathers rising from
its head. Although the bird looked very
majestic, she didn't like the way it was
clinging to the pole. It looked exhausted, as
though it might slip and fall at any minute.

'I think it needs help,' Ryan whispered.

'It's a ginormous eagle perched on a

church,' Isabelle said. 'How are we meant to help it?'

'I don't think it is an eagle,' Evie replied.

'Then what is it?'

'It's in trouble.' That was all Evie had to know.

Chapter 4

'We shouldn't all go up there, we might frighten it,' Ryan said. He knew a lot about animals, so Evie thought he was probably right.

'It's your idea to go eagle bothering,' Isabelle said.

Evie glided them all down to the ground.

The churchyard was dark and the stone angels looked ghostly in the moonlight. From here the bird on the weather vane could hardly be seen.

'I'll go,' she said. 'I think he might be hurt.'

'Be careful,' Isabelle warned. 'Eagles have sharp beaks, and talons.'

'It isn't an eagle,' Ryan replied.

'Well, it isn't a pigeon either,' Isabelle replied.

Evie grinned. She loved Isabelle and Ryan, but they could bicker for Britain some days.

She bounced on her heels a couple of times and then launched herself upwards. The black stone blocks that made up the walls of the church whooshed by as she raced up the side of the building. The tower narrowed to become a pointy steeple, like an ice cream cone tipped upside down. She stretched her arms out to slow down as she reached the weather vane.

Up closer the creature looked very sorry for itself indeed. Its feathers drooped and its head had fallen to its chest. She could hear it coughing and spluttering. It might once have been orange, or red, but sweat had turned its feathers dark brown, or black in the moonlight. It was about the same size as Myla, her dog, but it looked much, much lighter. Its thick feathers fluttered in the breeze. She was close enough to be able

to hear it breathe, long, laboured breaths as though it had a heavy cold.

Did birds catch colds?

She had no idea. But this was no ordinary bird. It looked like something from a fairy story, something that should be perched beside a powerful queen, or flying alongside winged horses.

'Er. Hello,' Evie said, trying to be polite. Maybe, if it was magic, it could talk. It was worth a try.

The bird lifted its head slowly and opened one weary eye. The whites of its eyes were red and sore-looking.

'Er. My name is Evie,' Evie said. She bobbed up and down on a sudden flurry of air. 'Can you, er, speak?'

The bird cooed softly. It sounded much more like a pigeon than an eagle. Then the coo turned into a heavy cough. The bird clutched tighter to the weather vane and let its head droop over the metal cockerel.

It looked terrible.

'I want to help,' Evie said, 'if I can? Would it be OK if I lifted you down? My friends are waiting down on the ground. They're nice. We can see if we can find a vet, or something for you.'

The bird sighed heavily.

Evie wasn't sure whether to take that as a yes, or no. So, she reached out, slowly, slowly, slowly, the way you were meant to do with frightened animals, and rested her hand on the bird's shoulder.

It felt warm, unnaturally warm, as though the bird had a fever.

Evie slipped her hand under the bird's wing. Then she lifted gently. The bird let go

46

of the steeple and let itself be cradled softly
in Evie's arms. 'There, there,' Evie said.
'You'll be OK.'

The bird really was much lighter than
an animal its size should be. She'd read
somewhere that bird bones were hollow,
and this bird felt so slight it was as though
there were nothing at all beneath its
feathers.

They both floated down to the ground
like sinking on to a cushion.

Isabelle and Ryan hurried over. In the
shadow of the yew tree, it was hard to see
the bird properly. It had settled on to the
ground in a bedraggled heap. It dropped its
head on to its wing and sighed again.

47

'What sort of bird is it?' Ryan asked, in wonder.

'And what's wrong with it?' Isabelle asked.

Evie stroked the bird's head. Whenever she felt ill, Mum or Dad would often do that and it always helped her feel better. 'We should take it to the vet. I can ask Mum to make an appointment.'

She was about the pick the bird up, to take it back to Mum, when Ryan put his hand on her arm.

'Wait,' he said. 'I've never seen a bird like this before, have either of you?'

Evie and Isabelle shook their heads.

'Well,' Ryan continued, 'do you think it might be a magical bird? A creature we can see because of the unicorn's gift?'

Oh. Evie looked at the glittering gold feathers, the flowing red tail. It didn't look like anything that usually turned up on Nana Em's bird table.

'Can other people see it, do you think?' Isabelle asked.

Evie shrugged. There was no one else in the churchyard that they could ask. It was late now, after all.

'The takeaway!' Isabelle said. 'Let's go there. I'm famished anyway.'

Evie was often a little unsure when it came to trusting Isabelle's ideas – they didn't always turn out the way she planned. But this seemed like one of Isabelle's better

ones. If the people in the takeaway could
see the bird, then they might help the bird
get to a vet. If they couldn't see the bird,
then they would know they were dealing
with magic.

Evie scooped the bird up, as gently as
she could manage. It moaned softly, then
dropped its head on to her shoulder and
sneezed: achoo, achoo, achoo.

It really was in a bad way.

They walked out of the church, under
a sombre archway. The road outside was
quiet. A bus trundled along in the distance,
a taxi sped past with its radio blaring.
Somewhere in the night a fox yowled.

Light spilled from the takeaway, warm

and friendly-looking. They crossed the road quickly.

The air smelled of frying and spices, with the tang of vinegar muddled in too. Ryan pushed open the door and they stepped inside. Evie cradled the bird gently in her arms. She felt it twitch as they moved into the warmth, but it didn't lift its head.

'Evening!' Behind the counter a man with a white hat on his head smiled at them. Behind him was a board covered in photos of food – kebabs, chips, pizzas, salads, all bright reds and yellows and greens. The man waved at the board. 'What can I get for you?'

Had he noticed the bird? Could he even see it?

It was right there, right in front of him, in Evie's hands. But she knew that grown-ups didn't always pay attention to important things that were right in front of them.

She stepped up to the counter, though she had to look up to see over it. In her arms, the bird raised its head slowly and stared at the man too.

'Is it all right to bring pets in here?' Isabelle asked loudly.

The man shook his head mournfully. 'Sorry, but no. Environmental Health would have my guts for garters. Have you got a dog with you? You'll have to leave it outside.'

The bird blinked slowly, once, twice, as though it couldn't believe what it was hearing.

Evie couldn't help but grin. The bird was poorly, but it was also magical. She was holding a real-live magical creature in her arms!

'A portion of chips, please,' Isabelle said, 'with red sauce.'

Chapter
5

The flight home was a little bit rocky. They all had to keep a tight hold on Evie, so that they didn't fall. But Evie needed two hands to carry the bird. And Isabelle insisted on carrying the chips.

'Hold tight!' Evie cried.

'I'm trying!'

'Stop twisting!'

'Watch out!'

They had a near miss with a flock of
seagulls, and Ryan lost a slipper somewhere
along the way, but they all made it back to
Isabelle's garden safely.

It was late now. All the lights in the house
were out. Isabelle held her finger up to her
lips – hush! But there was no need, the
others were silent as stones. No one wanted
to get caught in the garden in the middle of
the night.

The bird was curled up asleep in Evie's
arms. She could see his chest slowly rise and
fall as he breathed, his feathers glistening
in the moonlight. She hoped he would feel

better after some sleep.

'What should we do with him?' Evie asked softly, so as not to disturb the bird.

'There's no point calling a vet,' Isabelle said. 'You can't treat an animal you can't see.'

'Let's make him a bed in your room,' Ryan said. 'Maybe he's just exhausted from flying? My gran says a good night's sleep is the best tonic.'

Evie flew up, quite gracefully now, she thought, up to the open bedroom window. She rested the bird on Isabelle's bed while she popped down to collect the other two.

Isabelle clicked on her bedside light. In

the honey-coloured beam, the bird's feathers
glittered like warm jewels, iridescent with
rainbows. The plume of his tail was a
coppery fountain. He was beautiful. But his
eyes were closed and his breath was ragged.

'What should we do?' Evie asked. When
Myla or Luna was ill, Mum or Dad whipped

them round to the vet's quick smart.

But that was no good here.

'We should get him some water, and perhaps something to eat,' Ryan said. 'He might be exhausted, or starved. He might have been flying for hours.'

Evie looked doubtfully at the bird curled up on Isabelle's Hello Kitty duvet cover. 'What does he eat, do you think?'

Isabelle offered the nearly empty bag of cold chips to the bird. He didn't stir.

'Not chips!' Ryan said.

'Seagulls love them,' Isabelle replied, a bit huffily.

'Try corn, or peas,' Ryan said. 'That's what we take to feed the ducks.'

59

Isabelle nodded and slunk out of the room, on tiptoes, like a midnight-feast-ninja.

'Peas are fine for ducks, but he's not a duck, is he?' Evie asked.

She sank down on to Isabelle's bed. The bird nestled deeper into the duvet. There was a velvety, fleecy throw at the end of the bed. Evie pulled it up until the bird was cocooned in it. She thought she heard some gentle little snores come from under the covers.

'I don't know what he is,' Ryan said, 'I've never seen anything like him.'

'We must be able to find out.' She eyed the tablet beside Isabelle's bed. She wasn't sure how to search for something that she didn't have a name for. But there was no emergency librarian she could call in the small hours of the night.

She reached for the tablet.

The screen lit up. She opened the internet and started to search. Magical birds – that was a good start. She clicked on some images. Something from a film about a boy wizard. A page about fairywrens. Oh, they were cute. But she mustn't get distracted. There! There was a drawing of a bird that looked just like the one they'd found, but it was a more fiery red and orange. She clicked on the link, and gasped.

She heard the bedroom door open and shut, but she barely noticed – she was too busy reading.

Isabelle sneaked up soundlessly. She was
cradling a bowl of frozen peas. She laid
them down carefully on the bed, for the bird
to take.

He didn't move.

Not so much as a twitch.

'Oh,' Isabelle said sadly. 'He doesn't like
peas.'

'He wouldn't,' Evie replied. 'I've found out
what he is.'

'Well?' Ryan asked, trying to peer at the
screen over her shoulder.

'He's a phoenix.' She looked at the
huddled lump in the middle of the bed. It
shifted slightly, to get more comfy. 'It says
here they live to be a thousand years old.

And can shine as brightly as the sun.'

The lump in the bed sneezed.

'What do they eat?' Ryan asked. The
frozen peas were starting to thaw, turning
darker green and damp.

Evie read on. 'It doesn't say,' she said
doubtfully.

'What about getting sick? Does it say
anything about that?' Isabelle asked.

Uh-oh. It did. There was a whole paragraph about it in the encyclopaedia. As she read, Evie's tummy flipped over and her heart thumped loud enough to wake the house. 'It says they get sick when they're old. And there's only one thing that can help.'

'What's that?' Ryan asked.

'They have to bathe in fire,' Evie said. 'How on earth can we help with that? I'm not allowed to touch matches, not ever, not under any circumstances.'

'Me neither,' Ryan added.

Isabelle shook her head. 'My mum will let me do a lot of things, but starting a fire to let a bird have a bath in it? No way.'

Evie looked at the lump. It was still now.

It seemed to trust them and had settled down to sleep for the night.

How on earth were they going to help the phoenix?

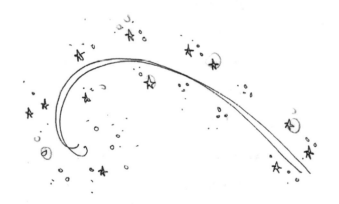

Chapter 6

Evie slept badly, worried about the phoenix. She could tell, from the muffled coughs and the restless turning, that the others felt the same way.

In the morning, after Isabelle's mum had stuck her head around the door to wake them, Evie went straight to the end of

Isabelle's bed. She pulled back the corner of the blanket.

'How is he?' Ryan asked.

'We should really give him a name,' Isabelle added. 'What about Red? Or Blaze? Or ... or ... Jeff?'

'Red is nice,' Evie said, only half listening. Red was still curled up tightly at the end of the bed. His head rested on his neatly folded wing. He opened one eye, very slowly.

The bowl of peas was still there, untouched.

'He looks worse,' Evie said. 'We have to work out how we're going to get a fire for him. There's a real fire in Nana Em's house, they use it in winter.'

Isabelle drew the curtains. Sunshine poured into the room. Bright green leaves danced on the trees outside. It was a lovely day.

'We haven't got a real fire in this house,' Isabelle said. 'Dad wanted underfloor heating downstairs, and it's all radiators upstairs.'

Ryan fished around in his overnight bag for his toothbrush. 'Well, I reckon we need to get dressed and ready, then go over to Nana Em's and see if she'll light a fire for us.'

It sounded like a plan.

After breakfast, and showers, and getting dressed for the day, Evie lowered Red into her backpack. It was a tight fit, but it just about worked. She left the zip open a tiny bit for fresh air. They walked together across the park. There were kids in shorts and T-shirts playing frisbee and five-a-side. The lake in the middle had small boats you could hire and splash about in. Magic twirled and danced, gold and sparkling, above all the happy people.

By the time they'd reached Evie's street, she was so warm, she had to wipe sweat off her forehead.

Nana Em's house was next door to Evie's.

'Hiya!' Evie yelled as she opened the front door. 'It's only me.'

'Evie, love,' Nana Em called from the back kitchen. 'What are you doing here, pet?' She came out into the hall, her hands dusty with

flour. 'I was just doing a spot of baking. Oh!
Here's Isabelle and Ryan too. How lovely.
You can help me eat the scones when I'm
done.'

They shuffled into the narrow hall. In the
front room, Evie could see the fireplace, with
photos of all the family on the mantelpiece,
and little china models of shepherds and
thatched cottages.

'Nana Em,' Evie said in her sweetest voice.
'Do you think you might light a fire for us,
please? It's a bit chilly.'

'Give over!' Nana Em laughed. 'It's hotter
than Spain here today.' She patted Isabelle's
arm. 'I went there last year with two old
school friends. It were a right giggle.'

Evie gripped the straps of her backpack
tighter. Red needed a fire badly. They had to
persuade Nana.

'Please,' she begged.

Nana Em frowned. 'You're serious? No,
Evie, I'm sorry, but it's just not a day for
that. It would be a waste. Come on, come
and help me with this scone mix.'

Evie trudged through to the kitchen, with the others behind her.

The back door was open and she could see Grandpa in the garden. He was pruning one of the bushes that had wild, lime green fronds shooting in all directions.

An idea blossomed in her mind. 'I'm just going to have a word with Grandpa,' she said.

'Hey up, Evie,' Grandpa said. 'What are you doing here?'

'Hi, Grandpa. What are you going to do with all the bits of plants you cut off?'

'They'll go in the compost,' he said, working quickly with his secateurs.

'Can you do a bonfire, instead?' Evie asked hopefully.

He tutted and shook his head. 'It's the wrong time of year. There's too much sap, it's all green wood, it's wick as a flea. No, autumn is the time for bonfires.'

Oh.

Evie took the backpack off slowly and cradled it in her arms. She sat down on the back step. Behind her, she could hear Isabelle and Ryan licking scone mix off a spoon, but she didn't want to go back inside. She'd failed and Red was the one who would pay for it.

'What's up, pet?' Grandpa asked. 'You wanted to toast marshmallows, is that it?'

'Something like that.'

He chuckled. 'This city used to be known

for its fires, did you know that? There were
foundries and furnaces and steel mills and
at night the sky would be lit up like daytime
with all the fires.' He tidied a few more stray
branches as he spoke.

'Was that when you were little?' she
asked.

'No, pet, it was before even my time. When my grandpa was a boy. Now most of the factories have been turned into flats, and you can only see the old furnaces in the museum.'

The museum? She felt an excited tingle.

'Does the museum keep the furnace hot, like in the old days?' Evie asked eagerly.

'I think so, yes. They keep the furnace in top condition and light it regular. Often as not, they do it during the holidays. Why, do you fancy a trip to the steel museum?'

'Oh, yes, please!' Evie said. She leapt to her feet and would have danced a little jig, if it weren't for Red getting bounced around in her backpack.

'I'm sure we can do that one day this week,' Grandpa said.

'Not today?' Evie gasped.

'No, not today. I've got to finish up out here and your nana has plans for us this afternoon.'

'Please can we go?' she begged. 'It's important.'

'I think we're free tomorrow,' Grandpa said. 'I'll check with Em, see what she says. Don't worry, the museum will still be there in the morning.'

Oh.

The museum might still be there, but would Red last that long? Evie peered into the unzipped top of her backpack. Red was

curled up, eyes closed, chest barely moving
as he breathed.

She hoped that he would hold on for
another day.

Chapter 7

Evie watched Red carefully all day, and a lot of that night. He slept mostly, curled up inside the backpack. She left him in her room, which was at the top of the house, away from noise and fuss. He didn't touch the bowl of water she left beside the open zip.

The next morning, Isabelle and Ryan were at her house at the crack of dawn, before Mum and Dad were even awake.

'We couldn't wait,' Isabelle said. 'How's Red?'

Evie shrugged her shoulders forlornly. 'Not good.'

'We need to get to the furnace right away,' Ryan said.

Grandpa was surprised to see them all as they bundled in through the back door into his kitchen. He was sitting at the small table, sipping tea. Nana Em was still in her dressing gown.

'Can we go to the museum now?' Evie asked.

Grandpa chuckled. 'You must be one of those early birds I keep hearing about. We can go as soon as it opens.'

'Can we be there for when it opens?' Isabelle asked.

'Fine. But let me finish my brew first. You can't ask a man of my age to be in charge of three young scamps without a cup of tea in him.'

They watched him finish his drink. They waited, impatiently, as he went upstairs to get ready. They tapped their feet at the sound of him singing in the bathroom.

'He's never coming,' Evie said. She held the backpack, with Red inside, very gently.

But Grandpa was ready eventually and

they all piled into his car, buckled up, and headed to the old steel works.

They pulled up outside the range of buildings that made up the museum. Most were low, honey-coloured brick, stained black. But there was one that had a huge chimney, like an extra room perched on top of the roof. A river ran past, turning a wheel to power the factory. Today the river glistened in sunshine and splashed merrily.

The reeds that stood like tufty exclamation marks along the water, swayed in the breeze.

There was no sign of smoke. No hint of a fire.

Not anywhere.

Evie turned about to check, but there was nothing.

Poor Red. Had they made this plan for nothing?

And then, from the huge chimney, came a tendril of grey smoke. A ribbon twisting in the air, before floating away.

'Looks like they've just sparked up the furnace,' Grandpa said in delight. 'We're just in time to see it catch.'

He strolled to the ticket office. Evie,

Isabelle and Ryan waited impatiently outside the furnace building.

As soon as they were allowed, they walked past the ticket collector, and found themselves in the centre of the foundry itself.

It was already warm, even though the fire had just been lit. The lights were low and the small windows let in hardly any sunshine. The space was gloomy and black, with shadowy figures peering at them from the darkness. Mannequins. There were shop mannequins, wearing old-fashioned clothes. What looked like old pokers and metal bars were arranged in displays like wet umbrellas in a stand. Labels and posters explained exactly what it all was. A recorded

soundtrack bellowed from hidden speakers
– the clang of metal on metal, the shouts of
workers, the hiss of molten steel. Evie felt a
fizz of excitement. It was like being in the
belly of a fiery dragon.

Where was the furnace itself? That's what
they needed if they were going to help Red.

She turned about the cavernous space,
trying to make out the shapes in the gloom.

There!

Set in one wall was a huge metal door,
black as night. In the centre of the huge
door was a smaller door, like a letter box,
for checking the flames. That little door was
open and an orange glow danced within.
They'd found the fire!

Evie was about to unzip her bag and let Red fly into the flames for his phoenix bath when she realised.

The little door was way too small for Red to fly inside.

'We need to open the main furnace door,' she whispered to Isabelle and Ryan. 'It's the only way for Red to reach the flames.'

A museum security guard stood beside the furnace. He wore navy trousers, a burgundy blazer and a very serious moustache. It was a bushy moustache. It was a dark moustache. It was the sort of moustache that said, 'Don't touch anything, don't run in the corridors, and whatever you do, don't even think about going near the furnace door.'

Amid the clanging steel and hiss of iron, the security guard was the scariest thing Evie had seen in a long time.

'We're going to need a distraction to get us past security,' Ryan said.

'Can't we just fly over his head and open the door?' Isabelle asked.

Evie looked across at Grandpa, who was

standing near an exhibit of metal lumps.
'I think if I flew up off the ground headed
straight at a fire, my grandpa would notice,'
she said.

Isabelle nodded. 'I suppose you're right.'

'There's another problem,' Ryan said
softly. His face was lined with a frown. 'The
catch for the furnace door is at the top. It's
got to be at least four metres off the ground.
Even if we do distract the guard, we can't
reach it.'

'Are you sure we can't fly?' Isabelle
pleaded. Evie knew she loved using magic
whenever she could.

But Grandpa was still in the room with
them. They couldn't distract Grandpa and

the security guard at the same time, could they? She watched Grandpa thoughtfully as he read the labels and posters. It might be possible …

'Wait!' Ryan said. 'I think I might have an idea. But we're all going to have to work together.'

He explained his plan, and Evie could have hugged him.

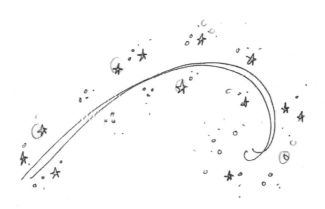

Chapter 8

Ryan, Isabelle and Evie – still carrying the backpack with Red inside – huddled into one of the dark corners of the furnace room to whisper about their plan. Grandpa was still poring over bits of steel as though they were delicious, hot slabs of lasagne.

The bushy-moustached guard – Boustache

for short – was still guarding the furnace door, as though he was a hairy sphinx guarding the pyramids.

Isabelle walked boldly up to one of the mannequins. It was a little plastic boy, dressed in old-fashioned clothes. He was pushing a heavy-looking cart and his face was set in a permanent frown. Isabelle lifted his brown flat cap from his head and plopped it on her own. 'Perfect!' she said very loudly indeed. 'I love museums with a dress-up section.'

'Oi!' Boustache growled like a bear with a sore throat. 'Put that hat back.'

Isabelle began unbuttoning the boy's waistcoat. 'It's just so much fun when museums have things for kids!' she said brightly.

Boustache looked at the furnace door. Then at Isabelle. Then at the door. Then at Isabelle who was buttoning herself into the navy waistcoat and posing like it was Paris fashion week. He growled like an angry bear with a headache and sore throat and stampeded over to her.

'PUT THAT BACK RIGHT NOW, YOUNG LADY!' he roared.

But Isabelle didn't put it back. Instead,

she whipped the floaty blouse-shirt thing up over the boy's head. Now he was just in his grey trousers, Evie felt a tiny bit sorry for him, but Isabelle was being a brilliant distraction.

Isabelle raced over to Grandpa. 'Here,' she yelled, 'it's for grown-ups too. This should fit!'

Isabelle leapt into the air and jammed the white top on to Grandpa's head. It covered his face like a veil, but it was way too small to go any further. Grandpa scrabbled at the fabric, yelping slightly. Boustache was right on her heels, but didn't know which of them to lunge for first – Isabelle in the cap and waistcoat, or Grandpa with a floaty white sack on his head.

Boustache decided on Grandpa. He roared
and grabbed for Grandpa's head. Grandpa,
unable to see his attacker, held up his arms,
kung fu style.

Isabelle was right in the middle of it all,
trying to shove the cap on to Boustache's
head now. 'Oh, that so suits you!' she cried.
'We should do a fashion show!'

Isabelle was the centre of attention and she wasn't about to let that change.

Ryan chuckled. 'Well done, Isabelle. Now it's our turn. You ready?'

Evie nodded. Isabelle's antics would buy them a few moments, but that was all. They had to move fast.

Together they raced towards the furnace. Even with the door still closed they could feel the heat coming from it. They couldn't get too close.

Evie's fists were screwed tight as she hoped and hoped and hoped that Ryan's plan would work. Was he really as good at darts as he thought?

Ryan reached for one of the long metal

poles that made up one of the exhibits. He hoisted it on to his shoulder, gripping the shaft tight. With his free hand out in front of him, he steadied himself, taking aim.

Then, he launched the pole up at the latch.

Evie could hardly bear to watch.

It sailed through the air, whizzing straight at the furnace. She gasped. The pole struck the latch squarely.

The clang reverberated around the gallery.

Then, everything happened at once.

The pole dropped to the floor and rolled into the shadows.

Isabelle screamed and threw a waistcoat, a hat, a blouse and – from who knows where – a pair of scruffy trousers into the air.

Grandpa and Boustache swivelled towards the sound.

And the furnace door fell open like a mouth, revealing the licking tongues of flame inside.

Evie dropped to her knees and tugged open her backpack. Red was curled up inside, head under his wing. 'Red, Red, the fire's right there,' Evie said urgently.

Would he move? Would he fly? She hoped he was well enough. With the adults watching, she couldn't fly him up there herself.

He didn't move.

'Please, Red, please. Now's your chance. You have to take it.'

Boustache was talking into his radio, saying something about a door failure, about needing back-up. About clearing the gallery. 'Everyone out,' he yelled. 'Everyone, up and out. Especially you!' He pointed at Isabelle.

'Please, Red, it's now or never,' Evie said.

Red lifted his head slowly. His neck uncurled like a leaf in springtime. Evie could feel warmth glowing from the fire, and, it seemed, Red could too. A shiver ran through his body. Then, for the first time since she'd met him, he stood up all by himself and fluttered awkwardly from the backpack.

'Out!' Boustache yelled, only metres away. 'Evacuate the building. Right now.'

Red turned his head towards the fire, it glowed like rubies and diamonds. His wings stretched weakly, like torn leaves.

'Go on,' Evie whispered, 'you can do it.'

Red breathed in the warm air. He beat his wings once, twice, then sailed upwards, gliding in a wide circle about the space, carried on the current of heat from the furnace.

Boustache and Grandpa couldn't see him at all. Grandpa slid his hand under Evie's elbow, thinking she'd fallen. She stood and, with Ryan and Isabelle, watched as Red turned towards the open door and the heartbeat of the fire. He sailed inside, a gold shape against the red.

Then, before they could see what happened to him, they were hurried out of the gallery by Boustache and the rest of the security team.

In moments, they were back in the gravel courtyard, surrounded by sand- and coal-coloured buildings. This time though, there was frantic activity and museum staff raced about, all trying to work out why the furnace door had opened by itself. That really wasn't supposed to be part of the experience!

'Let's just hope they don't find the metal pole,' Evie said worriedly. 'I don't want us to get into any more trouble.'

'It's all right,' Ryan said, 'I snuck it back

on to the display while Red was flying into the furnace. As far as the museum goes, it will stay a mystery.'

'Did everything go to plan?' Isabelle asked.

Evie looked up at the furnace building. The chimney still smoked, the fire was burning inside. Had it worked? Had they done the right thing for Red?

And then, in the midst of the swirling smoke, she saw a glint of gold. The sort of shimmering glittering light that meant magic was around. Then, shooting up from the chimney was the dazzling sight of a phoenix, strong and whole and full of life, trailing more gold magic behind him than

she had ever seen before – a comet of light.
Red! He launched into the sky, turning loop-
the-loops and figures-of-eight. Evie laughed
and clapped her hands together. 'Yes,' she
said, 'yes, everything went to plan.'

Chapter
9

They celebrated helping Red by having a
stop-over at Evie's house this time. Dad
made spag bol, which was one of his
specialities, and they spent the evening
rampaging around the garden with Lily,
Evie's little sister, and Myla the dog. Luna
the cat sat on top of the kitchen roof staring

down at them in horror at all the ruckus.

It took hours to fall asleep – everyone was still so excited. Mum had to come into Evie's room twice to say settle-down-some-of-us-have-work-in-the-morning.

When she did fall asleep – with Isabelle's toes in her face as they top-and-tailed in the bed – Evie dreamed about flying. She felt she was soaring through the inky black night against the diamond scatter of stars.

She woke suddenly, jerking awake with a feeling of falling.

The room was soft and still. She could hear Ryan, on the blow-up mattress on the floor, breathing gently. Isabelle made tiny, little snoring sounds at the other end of the bed. What time was it?

She looked at the alarm clock beside her bed. Five o'clock. Dawn. Thin fingers of sunlight reached around the blind in the skylight.

The wisps of her dream still hovered at the edge of her mind – flying over the rooftops and floating up to the clouds. The feeling of flying was the best ever. It was sad it was all over.

Then she saw the pale-blue flying bracelet
on the wooden tree by her bed, and Evie had
a delicious idea.

She shook Isabelle's big toe. 'Psst, Isabelle.
Isabelle, you awake?' Evie hissed.

'Wha?' Isabelle said grumpily.

'I was just thinking. Do you want to have
one last go of the bracelet? Shall we fly, one
last time?'

Isabelle was properly awake then. She
sat, bolt-upright, her hair all mussed from
sleeping and her eyes puffy. But she rubbed
them with her fists. 'You want to fly? Now?'

'Yes. Before the bracelet runs out. We've
still got time.'

Ryan rolled on to his side and opened his

eyes slowly. 'How long have we got?' he yawned.

Evie did some quick sums. 'We get given three days. And I didn't come to Isabelle's house until after breakfast three days ago. If it's five o'clock now, I think we've got at least four hours.' Then she glanced at the door. 'Though Mum has work, so we should be back in our beds before she wakes up.'

'We've got time?' Isabelle asked.

'We've got time,' Evie said.

'Yes!'

'Hush.'

'Sorry.'

They scrambled out of bed. They didn't bother getting out of their pyjamas, but they all pulled on shoes and jackets – it was chilly up in the air!

Evie had to stand right on tiptoe to pull the bar that opened the skylight. The opening wasn't very big – perhaps only enough room for one of them, two if they both breathed in tight. They wouldn't be able to go up all at the same time.

'You two go first,' Ryan said. 'I'll wait here. We can switch in a bit.'

Evie held Isabelle's hand tight. Then, she turned the bracelet on her wrist once, twice, three times … gold light twinkled free and Evie found herself floating upwards.

'Hurray!' Isabelle said, rising too.

'Still hush!' Evie warned – this would be

a terrible time for Mum to come into the room. They weren't in bed, they were above their beds. Mum wouldn't like it. She steered towards the open skylight and, with a rush of cold air, she and Isabelle were out, into the dawn light.

The city was even more magical than before.

Isabelle squealed in delight. The rising sun reflected off the glass of the tower blocks, making each pane look like gold fire. The sky was a beautiful baby blue, and peachy and pink, with one or two late stars still shining. It felt as though the whole world was new and fresh and waiting just for them.

Evie picked up speed, surging up into the
pale blue like a gull soaring for joy. The
vapour trails from high-up planes made a
ginormous game of noughts and crosses
above them.

'Woo-hoo!' At her side Isabelle spread
her arms wide. 'I'm Tinkerbell!' she yelled,
startling a nearby starling.

They swept over the street, watching
the cars like toys below and the buses like
wooden blocks – the city slowly waking up.

Evie and Isabelle flew until their cheeks
felt rosy with cold and their fingertips
were numb. It was glorious. Like birthdays
and Christmas and sports days and
holidays all rolled into one. And their

lovely city right there below them.

'It's probably Ryan's turn now,' Isabelle said with a sigh. It was clear she never wanted to stop. But fair was fair. They had to head back. The stars were all gone and the moon was so pale it looked as though it had been cut from tracing paper and stuck to the sky. There should be just enough time for Ryan to have a turn before they all needed to be tucked up back in bed when Mum got up.

As they dropped down towards the red tiled roofs of Javelin Street, Evie saw the little red van the postie drove trundling down the High Street. She waved at it. 'Thanks for bringing Grandma Iris'

presents, postie!' she yelled – he was far too
far away to hear!

She could see the skylight now, far below.
She'd need to concentrate if they were
to land neatly inside her room – without
bumping into anything and waking the
house.

But as she adjusted course, something
awful happened.

Gold light twisted around her and
was sucked back into the bracelet with a
whoomph. It all disappeared back where it
had come from.

Suddenly, there was nothing at all holding
them up. No magic, no warm currents of
air. Nothing.

They weren't gliding gracefully now. They were falling. Dropping faster and faster. The bracelet had failed! Magic had failed!

And they were plummeting towards the rooftops like stones.

Down.

Down.

Down towards the tiles.

Chapter 10

Evie could hear Isabelle scream, see
her open mouth. It was like being on a
rollercoaster as the car dipped into its
loop. Her stomach was in her throat. Wind
rushing past her ears. Isabelle gripped her
with both hands. Evie couldn't reach for
her bracelet.

The roofs were close now, getting closer. She could make out cracked tiles, mossy gutters, and spiky chimney pots.

Evie felt herself sob. But there was nothing she could do. Gravity had switched back on too soon. And it was going to hurt.

'Help!' Isabelle yelled.

But who could help them up here? No one, Evie thought.

And then, whoomph! Something soft and warm hit them from the side. It was gold, bright, glittering. Was it magic?

No.

They'd been bumped by golden feathers. They were both clinging to a broad,

copper-coloured back. Under her fingertips,
Evie could feel the stretch and pull of
strong muscles as the creature beat its
wings. *Red*. Red had caught them on his
back and now he was sailing up into the
morning sky with his wide wings spread

and his head held high. A fountain of
bright feathers burst like a crown from his
head.

'Red!' Isabelle cried, 'you saved us!'

Red squawked in reply, a low note that
tinkled with a sound like sleigh bells. His
cough was completely gone. He was strong
and whole again. Evie's heart thumped with
the tail-end of fear and the beginning of
delight.

Red was all better, and he had saved
them right when they needed it.

She wriggled to get properly on to Red's
back. Isabelle did the same. He didn't even
dip, as they moved. He was well enough
now to carry twenty little girls, it seemed.

Evie sank her arms around his neck and sank her head on to his back. He smelled of spiced smoke and sunshine. 'I'm glad you're better. Thank you,' she said.

He gave another musical squawk and swung around back in the direction of Javelin Street. Evie felt Isabelle's hand link around her waist, then her voice whispering in her ear. 'Evie, is this a dream? Am I really riding a phoenix?'

Evie giggled. 'You are! We are! Wheee!'

Red looped down fast, but caught an updraft off the roof and slowed to a hover. They were right above the skylight.

Inside the room, Ryan's face peered up, his eyes are wide as side plates. Isabelle

dropped down first. Ryan helped her
scramble through the open skylight. Evie
was next. When they were both safely back
inside her bedroom, Red gave one last
squawk and beat his wings, sailing up into
the bright morning.

Isabelle tumbled back on to Evie's bed.
'That was a-maze-ing,' she said, letting her
arms flop wide. 'The best ever.'

Evie looked at the floor. 'I'm sorry, Ryan.'

'What for?'

'You didn't get a turn flying. I don't know
what happened. The magic just stopped
working.'

Ryan reached up and clicked the skylight
closed. Then he sat in the chair beside her

desk and looked thoughtful. Evie didn't know what else to say – she felt bad he'd been here all alone.

'I wonder,' he said. 'When you came over to Isabelle's that morning, was that the first time you'd turned the bracelet on your wrist?'

She tipped her head sideways, staring at the sloping ceiling as she thought. 'No, I'd tried it right after the postie gave me the parcel. But nothing happened.'

'Something did happen, though,' Isabelle said, from the bed. 'Remember when you came to play darts – you were already off the ground.'

'You hadn't noticed you could fly!' Ryan

laughed. 'Only Evie could have a super
power and not even know.'

She felt herself blushing. Ryan was right.
The three days had started much earlier
than she'd thought. 'It was my fault we

fell, then, I got the time wrong,' she said to Isabelle.

'Maybe,' Isabelle replied. She sprawled over the whole bed, happy not to have to share it with anyone. 'Probably. But, it's also because of you that Red was there to save us. You got him down from the spire and you got your grandpa to take us to the museum.'

Ryan stood up, walked over and dropped his hand on Evie's shoulder. 'Yes. It's all down to you, Evie Hall. Since you came here, life has been three hundred times more interesting.'

'A million times more interesting,' Isabelle corrected.

Evie smiled shyly.

It was all of them, working together, that made it special, she thought. That, and a little dash of magic from Grandma Iris and her bracelets.

Evie
and friends

Evie

Full name: Evie Hall

Lives in: Sheffield

Family: Mum, Dad, younger sister Lily

Pets: Chocolate Labrador Myla and cat Luna

Favourite foods: rice, peas and chicken – lasagna – and chocolate bourbon biscuits!

Best thing about Evie: friendly and determined!

Isabelle

Full name: Isabelle Carter

Lives in: Sheffield

Family: Mum, Dad, older sister Lizzie

Favourite foods: sweet treats – and anything spicy!

Best thing about Isabelle: she's the life and soul of the party!

Ryan

Full name: Ryan Harris

Lives in: Sheffield

Family: lives with his mum, visits his dad

Pets: would love a dog ...

Favourite foods: Marmite, chocolate – and anything with pasta!

Best thing about Ryan: easy-going, and fun to be with!

What would be your

magic Bracelet

★ ☆ ♥ ☆ ♥ **power?**

Imagine you had your very own magic bracelet ...
find out which power would be yours!

What's your favourite item of clothing?

A. ❑ My ice skates.
B. ❑ Hard to choose – everything I own is black.
C. ❑ My puppy slippers!

Which animal is your fave?

A. ❑ Dogs – they're happy, whatever the weather!
B. ❑ Black cats.
C. ❑ Can't choose! I love all living creatures.

Your favourite colour is ...

A. ❑ All the colours of the rainbow.
B. ❑ Black. Yes, it's a colour.
C. ❑ Um ... soft cosy brown?

What's your favourite food?

A. ❑ Watermelon.
B. ❑ Dark chocolate anything.
C. ❑ Something I can share with
my furry friends – maybe a carrot?

I'm best at ...

A. ❑ Swimming, running, jumping …
B. ❑ Playing hide and seek.
C. ❑ Taking care of my pets.

And what's your fave weather?

A. ❑ All kinds!
B. ❑ Fog. Or mist.
C. ❑ A bright sunny day!

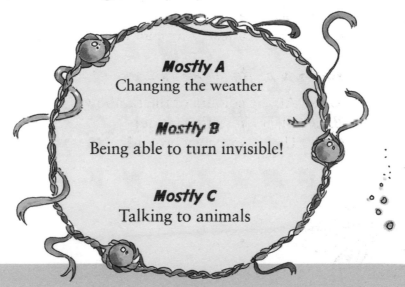

Mostly A
Changing the weather

Mostly B
Being able to turn invisible!

Mostly C
Talking to animals

Can you find all the words?

BIRD FLYING

FIRE MAGIC

ISABELLE EVIE

RYAN FRIENDS

BRACELET PHOENIX

C	I	E	M	R	U	U	B	X	E
K	J	W	P	J	G	R	A	I	R
E	L	L	E	B	A	S	I	N	Y
X	V	M	S	C	B	G	O	E	A
X	Z	I	E	D	N	I	S	O	N
S	C	L	E	I	N	Q	X	H	S
C	E	P	Y	F	M	E	B	P	J
T	G	L	I	M	A	G	I	C	G
V	F	R	D	R	I	B	A	R	T
V	E	C	J	G	V	W	D	B	F
L	G	M	X	K	A	N	V	V	N

C	I	E	M	R	U	U	B	X	E
K	J	W	P	J	G	R	A	I	R
E	L	L	E	B	A	S	I	N	Y
X	V	M	S	C	B	G	O	E	A
X	Z	I	E	D	N	I	S	O	N
S	C	L	E	I	N	Q	X	H	S
C	E	P	Y	F	M	E	B	P	J
T	G	L	I	M	A	G	I	C	G
V	F	R	D	R	I	B	A	R	T
V	E	C	J	G	V	W	D	B	F
L	G	M	X	K	A	N	V	V	N

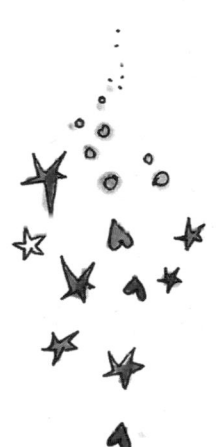

Jessica Ennis-Hill grew up in Sheffield with her parents and younger sister. She has been World and European heptathlon champion and won gold at the London 2012 Olympics and silver at Rio 2016. She still lives in Sheffield and enjoys reading stories to her son every night.

You can find Jessica on Twitter **@J_Ennis**, on Facebook, and on Instagram **@jessicaennishill**

Jessica says: *'I have so many great memories of being a kid. My friends and I spent lots of time exploring and having adventures where my imagination used to run riot! It has been so much fun working with Elen Caldecott to go back to that world of stories and imagination. I hope you'll enjoy them too!'*

Elen Caldecott co-wrote the Evie's Magic Bracelet stories with Jessica. Elen lives in Totterdown, in Bristol – chosen mainly because of the cute name. She has written several warm, funny books about ordinary children doing extraordinary things.

You can find out more at www.elencaldecott.com